THE DOORMAN

THE GIRL

POLICE OFFICER 1

POLICE OFFICER 2

THE MANAGER

ISBN 978-09974493-6-5

Published by
AMPERSAND, INC.
515 Madison Street
New Orleans, Louisiana 70116

719 Clinton Place
River Forest, Illinois 60305

www.ampersandworks.com

Design: David Robson

Printed in U.S.A.

To request a personalized
copy or to schedule a book
signing/school reading email
info@turtledetectives.com

www.turtledetectives.com

DEDICATED TO

Helen and Bill Munson: Mom and Dad.
Every moment of yours was mine.
Every word of mine is yours.
—ELAINE LOESER

My wife and kids, who are my partners in crime.
And my mom, who raised me right.
—GREG ARVANITAKIS

The Case of
THE PINCHED STRADIVARIUS

The Adventures of MILES AND FARGO: Turtle Detectives™

Written by ELAINE LOESER • Illustrated by GREG ARVANITAKIS

AMP&RSAND, INC.

Chicago • New Orleans

LOOK!

 I'm not moving.

 No, really, look.

HEY, STOP!

STOP, THIEF!

HEY GUYS... WHAT GOT INTO YOU?

 Mom, mom. That guy knocked that little girl down and stole her curvy box.

 She's crying. Her knee's bleeding.

Forget it. Nobody can hear us.

 I thought dogs had good hearing.

 **They don't even know we're alive.
They have no senses at all.**

 **Why do they call them man's
best friend, and not us?**

 **Cuz we're cold and wet
and they're warm and fuzzy.**

 We're not cute?

 We're smart, that's different.

THE
N EX T
→
DAY

Z Z

! ?

FARGO... YOU'RE SUPPOSED TO LET MILES SIT THERE TODAY.

The Daily Daily

 Fargo, look.

 Take a hike.

 It's the little girl. From yesterday.
In *The Daily*.

 What's a Stradivarius?

 The curvy box, I guess.

 So what's "prodigy"?

 It sounds smart.
And she looks smart to me.

The Daily Daily $1.00

STRADIVARIUS
PINCHED FROM KID PRODIGY

A thief made a big grab from a little girl today when her violin was snatched right out of her small hands as she walked home from school. Police have no description of the culprit at this time. The girl only saw him from the back. "He was a fast runner," she said. There were no other witnesses, but cops hold out hope that someone in one of the surrounding buildings saw something.

The Prodigy and her prize violin

High – 85
Low – 68

Business - Section 2
Sports Wrap Up - Section 3

You thought the Super was smart and he blew the fuse on our filter.

 That Super owes us a new filter.

 I've gotta go get a new filter for your tank. This one stopped working for some reason.

 The Super broke it, Mom.

 Bye, boys.

 Look at those stupid dogs. Nothing to do but sleep.

What's up there?

Green stuff, floating in water.

I was right. They don't know we're here.

Who's up there?

You think they heard us?

They heard *me*, not you.
Jump in and say something.

Hey dogs. How's it going?

 Come over here and talk by the new filter.

 What are you guys?

 We're turtles.

 How long have you been here?

 We're prehistoric—we've been here forever.

 I mean in New York.

 Long as you. We all came together.

 Wow. Who knew?

Time for our walk.

 Hey, listen you guys.
Could you do us a favor outside?

 What? We're in a hurry.

 Go across the street and take a look around.
A good long look.

 Bogie always does that.

 Look for what?

 For a guy in a tee shirt with a rat on it.
A big rat.

 That's a subway tee shirt. Very common.

 Whatever. Tall guy, gym shoes.
Hat with a little brim.

 Hipster, they call that—on the street.
Those hats.

 Tattoo on his wrist.

 I didn't see a tattoo.

 It's a bulldog. Ugly.

 I hate bulldogs.
One tried to eat me in our lobby.

 So be careful out there.

 Who's ready to go?

 They're useless.

 I don't see them.

 Me neither.

 You think they were confused?

 Of course they're confused. They're dogs.

 We gave you orders.

We don't take orders. We're dogs.

Dogs take orders.

WHERE WERE YOU?!
WE WERE WATCHING...

NOT. BICHONS.

 Mom didn't want to go that way.

We went by the Ritz Hotel and got treats instead.

It's him! The doorman. He did it.

 Look at him being nice to that old lady.

 She'll be next.

The Daily Daily

$1.00

STRAD STILL GONE

Girl In Pickle

Cops are strung out over the theft yesterday of a priceless fiddle, as the trail grows cold. The daring daylight grab took place blocks from the school where its pigtailed prodigy had just played a concert for World Peace. The rare Stradivarius belongs to a museum, and is on loan to the cherub. It is one of only 30 of its kind in the world.

Page 2

 Is that English?

 Stradivarius that means.

 Pickles are green—like us.

 That poor little girl.
Her violin cost two million dollars.
And it's on loan.

MOM! WE KNOW
WHO DID IT!

KEEP YOUR EYES OPEN ON OUR WALK, BOYS. YOU'RE GOOD LITTLE DETECTIVES.

 Is she kidding?

 Love is blind.

 Bogie. Bogie. The doorman did it.

 Did what?

 Just go over where we told you and get into that closet behind the doorman.

 What's in the closet?

 Dog treats.

 We're on the case.

 You lied to them.

 For the greater good.

There they are.

 Mom's talking to the doorman.
She's laughing.

 Mom's too nice.

 Look at Bogie.
He's getting into that bush by the door.

Management doesn't like dogs by the shrubs.

Bogie. No. Come over by me.

He kicked Bandit!
The doorman kicked Bandit in the face.

 Mom won't let him get away with that.

 Bandit's crying.

 It's an act. You've seen them.

 Mom's calling that cop over.

 Look in the closet, Mom. The closet.

That's the violin that was stolen. Look.

 Stand back, everybody. This is a crime scene.

TWO DOGS
SNIFF OUT STRAD

Doorman Pinched in Collar

Cops, aided by two sharp-witted, crusading dogs, recovered the pinched Stradivarius on loan to a pigtailed prodigy. The dogs sniffed out the callous criminal and brought him to heel without regard for their own safety.

One dog suffered minor injuries during the capture. "Without the help of these two noble canines, we would never have found that fiddle," Officer Grumpki said. The building where the culprit worked does not allow dogs.

Cast of Characters

 **FARGO**

 **MILES**

 **MOM**

 **BANDIT**

 **BOGIE**